THEIR HYBRID

SKYE MACKINNON

Peryton Press

Their Hybrid © Copyright 2019 Skye MacKinnon

All rights reserved under the International and Pan-American Copyright Conventions. No part of this book may be reproduced or transmitted in any form or by any means, electronic or mechanical, including photocopying, recording, or by any information storage and retrieval system, without permission in writing from the publisher.

This is a work of fiction. Names, places, characters and incidents are either the product of the author's imagination or are used fictitiously, and any resemblance to any actual persons, living or dead, organizations, events or locales is entirely coincidental.

Cover by Peryton Covers.

skyemackinnon.com

Created with Vellum

BLURB

**She was born to serve.
Pity she doesn't want to.**

DX-4, also known as Dex, is a hybrid: not quite human, not quite machine. She spends her days running errands for her three masters, until one day she ends up in a bit of a pickle.

Meaning she could be killed for what she did.

Her masters try everything they can to help her, but will it be enough? And is her heart human enough to return their love?

A steampunk reverse harem novella set in a dystopian world.

CHAPTER 1

"Turn right at that junction. Watch out for strays."

Yes, I know. It's not like I haven't walked this route every day for the past five years. But still, Dan tells me what to do. He's very controlling in a way, but in a kind way. He's protective of me, I think. Although maybe that's just wishful thinking. I'm their property, after all, of course he's interested in keeping me safe.

"Careful, there's something on the ground just ahead of you."

Yes, I can see that. It's a rat, dead and bloated. I cringe as I step over it, trying not to breathe in the foul air. Sometimes I wish I could transmit more than just my sight to my masters. They don't know how the city smells and reeks. Maybe they'd not make me go out as much if they knew. But of course, they don't, and they likely never will.

I walk faster, wanting to get out of this area as soon as possible. Not that my destination is any more pleasant, but there are less dead animals on the pavements in the Green Zone. The unpleasantness there isn't obvious. In fact, it's probably the cleanest and nicest looking part of the city. Instead, the corruption lies beneath the surface, beyond the polished windows.

I shiver as I think of the man I'm going to see. I wish my masters wouldn't force me to.

"Dex, there's something on the lens."

I huff and wipe the lens of my implanted eyecam with my soiled shirt sleeve. Not sure it's going to make a difference, but I can't actually see through that eye. Only my masters can. I have one human and one mechanical eye. I don't remember if I ever had two human eyes, but it doesn't matter. Dwelling in the past is useless, I've learned that a long time ago.

"That's better. Thanks, Dex."

I smile at Dan's nickname for me. My real name is DX-4, but he found that too boring, so he turned it into Dex. I like it. It almost makes me feel like a real person, someone with a proper name and identity.

I continue my walk, knowing that I'm getting ever closer to my destination. The grime and stink of the Brown Zone are getting lesser and I can see trees in the distance. The only trees in the entire city. The people in the Green Zone are the richest of the rich, the only ones who can escape the smog-covered areas and live amongst nature. I'm sure most of the dwellers in the lesser zones have never even seen a tree, let alone touched one. Or even breathed the clean air that I'm beginning to feel on my face.

A large iron gate separates the Green Zone from the rest of the city. There are two Watchers on duty and I sigh in relief when I notice that neither of them is a full human. Us hybrids are on the same level, Watchers or not, but the pure humans always think they're above us. Well, they are. Everybody knows that. They made us, after all, which is why they feel they can do whatever they want to us. And being a female hybrid about to enter a zone full of pure humans... it's not an ideal situation. No matter how highly they think of themselves, some humans are predators. Evil. Dangerous.

My masters are aware of that, but they can't do anything about it. They can see through my mechanical eye and they can hear what I do, but that's it. They can't fight attackers off for me. They can't protect me when darkness falls and the city's unsavoury characters crawl onto the street. No, I'm on my own.

"What do ya want?" one of the hybrids asks, his metal eyebrows raising at the same time as his mechanical lips open and close. He's definitely more than half metal. His colleague looks mostly human though, if it wasn't for the mechanical arm that is now pointing a revolver at me.

"I'm here to see Mr Bradley on behalf of my masters."

I hand them my ID plate which contains all the information they require. If they are clever enough to access it. Not all of the hybrids are. I sometimes wonder if the conversion has a negative effect on the brain, or if they were stupid before.

The guy with the metal arm takes my ID and disappears into the tiny guardhouse while the other one watches me curiously. They must be new. I come here most days; usually the guards know me.

His metal eyebrows twitch as he's trying to figure out why I'm here. Not many hybrids are allowed into this zone. It's reserved for humans, mostly. The only hybrids in here are servants. Not that they get paid, but most humans don't like using the word 'slaves'. It makes them sounds bad, so they keep referring to us as servants.

"What's the hold-up?" Dan asks and I wipe the lens of my eye again. Can't he see that the hybrid is still in the guardhouse?

He sighs. "It's getting dark soon, you shouldn't be out there for much longer."

I look at the large clock tower in the distance, barely visible behind the rows of pretty brick houses. Almost four. With all the smog, it gets dark at five, sometimes even earlier. It's rare nowadays that the smoke lifts its grip on the city. We live in perpetual dusk that drives many people mad.

"It seems all is in order," the second hybrid says in a deep voice, handing me back my ID. "You have two hours in the Zone, don't stay here for longer than that."

He gives me a smile and I look at him in surprise. People don't smile in the Green Zone. Especially not hybrids. He's most definitely new.

I nod at him in return and wait for the gate to open.

It's the same screech as every time. They should really oil it for once. But most people living in the Zone never leave. They send their servants or hybrids out to get them things. Or have stuff delivered - which is precisely what I'm doing right now.

I hurry along the brick roads like so many times before. I could do this in my sleep, if I *did* sleep. I vaguely remember what that was like, but it's only a fleeting memory.

At the end of a narrow close on my right is Mr

Bradley's house. It's large and imposing, with big windows that seem to stare at me from afar.

He's one of the richest men in the city, if not the richest, so he can afford a home this size despite the housing crisis. He's got dozens of hybrid servants and guards, all made by Bradley Enterprises, the same company that created me. He called himself my father, once, and it still creeps me out. Hybrids don't have parents.

I use the large lion knocker, banging it hard against the brass door. Only seconds later, a servant opens the door and waves me inside. They've probably seen me approach, or the hybrids at the gate have notified them. Either way, I am led straight into Mr Bradley's dining room, where he's waiting for me. He's eating a massive lobster that's far too big for the plate it sits on. Breaking apart one of the claws with a crunch, he ignores me and focuses on his dinner instead. I'm tempted to check my pocket watch for the time. I can't stay here for long.

Finally, once he's eaten the meat in the lobster claw, he turns to me with a smile.

"How much do you have?"

"One pound, as agreed," I answer stiffly, dreading what's to come.

His eyes turn greedy as he gets up and comes towards me. I'm tempted to back away but I know there's no escaping this.

"Arm," he commands and I hesitantly stretch out my right arm. It's the metal one; the one that is the most non-human part of me. He grips my elbow tight and with a quick twist, he detaches the metal part from my upper arm. I bite down a scream; it hurts the way he does it. My masters are much more gentle; they do it slowly and carefully. Mr Bradley doesn't care about my pain.

He opens a hidden latch and turns the arm over, emptying the contents onto the mahogany table. One pound of finest opium powder in an iron cylinder. It's what my masters trade in, it's how they sustain themselves. Chained to their house, unable to breathe in the toxic air, they've become traders - in illicit things, mostly. This opium was likely supposed to end up with someone else, but they substituted the real stuff and took a pound for Mr Bradley. It's how they pay for me.

Of course you can buy opium on the streets - almost every shop in the lesser Zones sells laudanum - but this is different. It's pure, undiluted, of the highest quality. The stuff usually reserved for royalty.

Mr Bradley isn't royal, but he likes to think he is. I'm not sure he even takes the opium himself; maybe he only offers it to guests to show his wealth.

I've seen opium dens before, dark places where men search for oblivion; full of smoke, sweat and broken dreams. It's only the lower classes who frequent those dens. I can't imagine Mr Bradley lying on a stained mattress, drooling as he babbles about his lost love.

He carefully opens the cylinder and inspects the opium. It's an ochre powder and looks no more harmful than pepper. Sadly, I've seen the effect it can have on people. They get emotional, relive old memories, become corpse-like dreamers. And some become overly friendly with the hybrids working in some of the dens.

Mr Bradley takes a bowl and empties the opium into it, before weighing it on a beautiful set of bronze scales.

"It's not enough." He grabs me by the shoulder and

pulls me close until he's looking straight into my eyecam. "It's not enough," he repeats.

"Tell him it's exactly one pound, as agreed," Luke's deep voice comes through my earpiece.

I do as my master tells me, even though I know that Mr Bradley won't believe it.

"Look at the scales, it's not a pound!"

Mr Bradley shoves me towards the table and bends me down until my eyecam is pointing at the scales. He's right, it's an ounce less than what it should be. I can't believe that it's my masters' fault though. Maybe Mr Bradley manipulated the scales?

He roughly turns me around again so he can be seen through my eyecam.

"I demand extra payment," he growls. "Two hours with this hybrid should do."

I gasp at his suggestion. He's still holding me uncomfortably tight, his face far too close to mine. I've always found him repulsive, but today he's become outright creepy.

"Don't worry, Dex," Dan says calmly. "We'll find another solution."

"Tell him we'll send an extra ounce next time," James instructs and Luke makes an approving sound. All three of them are watching what's happening. In a way, that's reassuring, but it also doesn't help me in the slightest. They're not here and they won't be able to protect me from Mr Bradley. No, I have to do that myself.

"They're saying they'll send an extra ounce tomorrow," I tell him, but he shakes his head.

"Not good enough. They had their chance, they blew it. I'll take you as payment today, and if they don't send at least two more ounces tomorrow, I'll get to have you again."

I shudder at the thought. There are entire hybrid brothels for men who prefer hybrids over real women - or who can't find a woman - but thanks to my masters, I've never been exposed to any such thing.

And now Mr Bradley is looking at me in that strange way, his mouth opening...

I knee him in the balls. It's not even the leg that's been reinforced with metal, but he cries out nonetheless, clutching his crotch with both hands, jumping up and down. It would be funny if it... well, if it wasn't.

"Guards!" he shouts, his voice suddenly high pitched rather than the deep baritone he usually has.

I grab my metal arm and run, just about managing to evade his grasp.

People are running down the creaky staircase, but I'm already halfway out of the house, fleeing for my life. I run and run, along the street I just came from, ignoring the windows opening all around and the people staring down at me. Some are cheering me on, others are starting to throw things at me.

But I run on, towards the gate, tears running down my cheeks.

Did I just destroy my masters' livelihood?

CHAPTER 2

By the time I get back home, it's grown dark. The street lamps are illuminating the smog wafting through the narrow lane and I wrap my scarf closer around my face. I don't want to breathe in too much of the city's poisonous air. It's worst now in the summer when the heat gets trapped between buildings, warming the dust and dirt on the streets. It's not a nice place to live, not at all. Often, I wish I was living somewhere else, out in the countryside, but as a hybrid, you live wherever your masters live. And in my case, I should call myself lucky that their house is in the outskirts of the city. Far enough out that the air doesn't kill them, close enough that they can afford it. Living in the city is cheap; the more crowded, the less you have to pay. My masters aren't poor, but they're also nowhere near as rich as the people living in the Green Zone. They could be earning more if their health was better, but that's not something that can be changed.

All three of them have the same lung condition, and

even just walking outside in the smog for a few minutes makes them cough terribly. They could die from it, so they stay inside, trapped in their own home, conducting business from there. That means they either have to ask their clients to come to them, or they send me. Which is why I'm running between their house and the Green Zone every day, doing errands. It's not always bringing things to Mr Bradley; sometimes it's just sending telegrams or getting money from the bank.

They didn't buy me; they're not the type of people to buy a slave. I was a gift from an associate, and they took me in rather than have me go to someone not as kind as themselves. I'm grateful for it; I have a good life with them.

My masters' house is at the end of a narrow close, an anonymous door on a long row of houses. They all look the same. It's a boring neighbourhood, but my masters don't have to see what's around them. For them, the inside is what matters, and they've done that up as good as they could.

I unlock the door - they always keep it locked even when they're in - and quietly walk up the carpeted staircase leading to the living quarters. Downstairs is the office and storerooms, upstairs is where we live. Where they live. I have a bed in the attic.

They've not said anything while I was running home. Does that mean they don't want to see me? They must be terribly displeased. I may have cost them everything.

I sneak along the corridor leading to the attic trapdoor, making as little noise as possible.

"We know you're here!" a deep voice calls out from the living room and I sigh. Of course they do. They always know where I am; they can see it for themselves through the camera embedded in my skull.

If I had a tail, I would now be walking with it hanging between my legs.

I enter the living room, opening the door just wide enough to slip inside.

All three of my masters are there, sitting by the fireplace. It's summer, but they have it on nonetheless. 'A home without a fire isn't a home', Dan likes to say. Mr Daniel, I correct in my head. I shouldn't be calling them by their nicknames while I'm in the same room. It might slip out and distort our relationship even further. I'm just a hybrid, made to serve humans. I'm not supposed to be friends with them.

"Dex, come on in," James says quietly but firmly. I shut the door behind me and take a few steps inside, not sure what to do. There are only three large armchairs in the room, and all three of them are currently occupied by my masters.

Dan, James and Luke. Three brothers, so similar they could almost be triplets. Maybe they are, they've never told me. And why would they...

All three of them have dark, almost black hair, but while Luke tames his in a ponytail, the other two have theirs cut short. Dan's hair is a little curlier than James's and I wish he'd let it grow so I can see the curls. They are clean-shaven as always and meticulously dressed in dark suits, complete with waistcoats and pocket handkerchiefs.

They look ready to go to a dinner party, but sadly, they never do. I've heard stories of how they did leave the house occasionally when they were younger, taking a carriage that would mostly protect them from the air, but they don't anymore. Even though they're my masters and a lot more important than I am, I sometimes pity them.

"We've talked about what happened," James begins slowly and my heart begins to beat faster. "And we all agree that you did the right thing. He had no right to treat you like that or threaten what he did."

"We feel terrible because we exposed you to danger," Dan adds. "I know it's dangerous in the city, and you have to go out there every day, but I hope you know we wouldn't make you do that if we could do it ourselves. One of us is always watching though, and we do have measures in place to help you should something happen."

"You do?" I ask in surprise.

Dan smiles gently. "Of course we do. You're our Dex, we wouldn't just leave you out there."

I smile back. A warm feeling is spreading through my belly. They actually care for me. I always tried to ignore the signs because I didn't want to be disappointed, but here they are, telling me that they'd find a way to rescue me. Not that I'd need rescuing. I'm strong, independent and smart. That's the way I was made.

"But back to the matter at hand," Luke says in his deep, melodic voice. It's like dark chocolate got together with sweet honey. I could listen to him all day. It's always a treat when he's the one at the microphone, giving me instructions. Sometimes he starts talking about his life, about things he read, anything really to pass the time. He gets bored quickly, I think.

"We cannot send you back to Mr Bradley, not with

what he threatened to do, and not after you hurt his crown jewels."

Dan splutters into the teacup he'd just lifted to his mouth.

"This is serious, Dan," Luke admonishes his brother. "He might ask for Dex to be punished. A hybrid attacking a human is a grave offence. The good thing is that he wasn't hurt badly, but still, it's his right to demand retribution."

The warm feeling in my belly disappears instantly. The laws are clear; a hybrid committing a crime against a human can be punished severely. Switched off, even. Luckily, the hybrid's owners have a say in what happens, but even so... I don't want to die.

Nervously, I fumble with the straps holding my corset in place. They've become loose while I was running, but it's still tight enough to stay on until I go to bed. From the beginning, my masters allowed me to wear human clothes. Some hybrids are forced to wear simple one-piece jumpsuits, but my masters bought me an entire wardrobe full of corsets, beautiful dresses, capes and even some breeches for errand days when a skirt would get in the way. If I didn't have my metal modifications, I could almost pass as human in these clothes.

"He wanted to rape her," James growls, pulling my mind back to the conversation. "He should be the one to be punished."

"It doesn't work that way," Luke says sadly. "Hybrids don't have rights and you know that. And by the time the petition in parliament is being discussed, it will be too late."

"A petition?" I ask, not having heard of that before.

"Yes, we got together with a few other gentlemen and petitioned parliament to establish a basic charter of rights for hybrids."

"Why didn't you tell me?" I'm trying to keep my voice level but it's quivering slightly from both excitement and hurt that I didn't know about this.

Dan smiles. "It was supposed to be a surprise."

The sound of the door knocker makes us all jump a little. It's late; most people stay in their homes after darkness falls. It's not safe out there, at least not for decent folk.

I automatically turn to go downstairs, but James stops me.

"Let me. It might be him."

I shudder and let him pass, waiting with bated breath as he walks down the stairs and opens the door. He's talking to several men, but I can't hear what they're saying.

I shriek as a hand touches my shoulder.

"Sorry," Luke mutters, but he doesn't remove his hand. He gently squeezes my shoulder and I freeze, the sensation being so new and strange. Hybrids don't get touched like that. Not in that gentle, reassuring way. He's touching me like he would a friend...

I force myself to relax and enjoy the feeling of his warm hand. If I focus on him, I can forget about the men downstairs, the men who might be here to take me away.

The door falls shut with a bang and a moment later, James is back in the living room, slightly out of breath from running up the stairs. None of them gets much exercise, being penned up in their house.

"Was it them?" Luke asks, pulling me a little closer.

James nods grimly. "I managed to persuade them to give us until tomorrow to hand her over." When he sees my expression, he adds quickly, "Not that we'll do that, of course."

I shake my head and step away from Luke's touch. "You have to. You can't lose your business with Mr Bradley because of me. He's your most profitable client, I'm not worth it."

Suddenly, James is in front of me, holding me by my arms and forcing me to look into his dark blue eyes. "Don't you ever say that again. You're worth a thousand Mr Bradleys. We're not giving you to him, never."

"Let me look something up... I'll be in the library," Dan mutters and leaves the room without further explanation. I'm left with Luke and James, both of them closer to me than I'm used to. I think I like it.

"Did they say what they wanted with me?" I ask quietly and James's grip on me tightens.

"They cited a clause in our buyers' contract," he says reluctantly. "Because you were made by Bradley Enterprises, attacking Mr Bradley has more serious consequences than if he was another human. They want to decommission you."

"No way!" Luke shouts, putting his hand back on my shoulder, squeezing hard, almost possessively.

I'm beginning to feel really afraid. My masters are good men, but they aren't powerful like Mr Bradley. They have no way to resist him. They don't have enough money to bribe him, they don't have political influence, and the friends they have in high society will likely not understand the problem. Most of them have hybrids, but from what I've heard, I'm the only one who gets treated like a human.

I'm amazed they found enough people to start a petition. But as they said, by the time Parliament debates it, it'll be too late for me. I'll be an empty shell, my mind ripped from my body.

"I'll run," I whisper. "They can't punish you for that."

"No way," James says firmly. "Lone hybrids are captured and returned to their maker. You'd end up with Bradley Enterprises, same as if we gave you to them now."

I feel like apologising to them again, but I can't. Mr Bradley had no right to do what he did. Well, he had every right, because us hybrids don't have rights. But it's wrong, morally wrong, and I can't stand for that. I'm not going to sell my body that way. Not even for my masters.

Being a hybrid means that I'm both human and machine. I have feelings; I can feel pain. And Mr Bradley would have given me a lot of pain, no doubt about that. He's that kind of person.

"Sit down, I'll make us some tea," Luke says gently and pushes me towards one of the armchairs. I'm too confused to enjoy the experience of being in one of their comfy chairs.

I need to run. I can't get my masters involved in this. They're too kind, too nice. They've given me a good life so far, and I'm probably one of the happiest hybrids in the city. At least I was, until today.

But James is right, hybrids walking around without their masters' identification get captured. Not all are returned to their maker as he said, some get traded on the black market or dismantled for parts. I shudder and

James mistakes that as me being cold, pushing my armchair closer to the fire.

Luke presses a mug of hot tea into my hands and they both take a seat on the other two chairs. Did it really take Mr Bradley to bring us all together like this?

Before I can even take the first sip of tea, Dan runs into the room, waving a book in his hand.

"I've found a way!"

CHAPTER 3

"No way," I protest. "It's not right."

"Why not? It'll only be on paper, we don't expect anything from you."

"I couldn't do that to you."

James sighs in exasperation. "Have you ever seen any women visiting us?"

I shake my head. Strangely enough, no.

"That's because we're not interested in any of those giggly girls flaunting around the city's ballrooms. We like real women."

I laugh bitterly. "I'm neither real nor a woman."

"But you are!" James goes on his knees in front of me. "You are the most beautiful woman I know," he says softly.

"And the bravest," Luke adds.

"And the brightest," Dan chimes in.

My cheeks heat with embarrassment, but I refuse to listen to their flattery.

"No, I forbid you to throw your lives away like that."

Dan laughs heartily. "And that's exactly why we want to marry you."

I cringe at the word. It's their brilliant idea, so they think. Dan found a reference to a slave owner marrying his slave, freeing her in the process and making her an equal member of society. They believe that they can use the same law to make me one of them. Human, at least on paper. Britain doesn't have a constitution and relies on case law. As there are no law cases about hybrids, maybe those mentioning slaves will apply. That's the theory.

"You keep saying 'we'," I protest. "Last time I checked, polygamy was illegal in Britain."

James chuckles. "We'd have to decide on one of us to be on the marriage certificate. But you know us, we like to share. We do everything together, so I can't imagine us having three different wives."

Luke shudders in mock horror. "I'm sure I couldn't stand them."

"Let's draw lots," Dan suggests. "Or we could do paper, scissors, stone."

"Wait, I still haven't agreed yet!" I tell them with a stern glance. As flattering as it is for them to want to marry me, this is wrong on so many levels. And that's exactly what I tell them.

"First, that law was for slavery, not hybrids."

"What are hybrids if not slaves?" Luke mutters but I ignore him.

"Second, you are three dashing young men who will no doubt find one or more perfect wives at some point. You don't want to waste that opportunity."

"I don't want another wife," James complains.

"Third, you don't want to start a fight with Mr Bradley.

He's powerful, he won't just let this go."

"He won't be able to touch you once you're married to us, and we'll find a new buyer. This country is addicted to opium, we've only scratched the surface," Dan argues.

"Fourth, who would marry us at this time of night? It would have to be in the next few hours before Mr Bradley's men come again tomorrow morning."

Dan grins cheekily. "That's easy. There are certain advantages of having a priest as your godfather."

I sigh in frustration. Why do they need to have an answer for everything?

"Fifth, we're not in love."

That shuts them all up.

Until James says, "Neither were our parents, but they fell in love shortly after they got married. They never had the chance for romance before. Sometimes that needs time. And even if not, as we said, we don't expect any... marriage duties from you. Everything can be as it is now, except that we won't expect you to run errands for us. We'll get a new servant, a human this time, not a hybrid. And the four of us will live here together, happily ever after."

"But what will your family say?" I ask weakly, hating and loving them for finding a solution to all my arguments. "What about your friends?"

"They'll have to accept it," Luke says coolly. "If they don't, then they're not worth being part of our lives anyway."

I get up and take a stand in front of them, putting my hands on my hips and looking at them sternly. I'm trying to do a matron impression but I'm not sure if it's working.

"Now listen to me. You're not going to throw your lives

away like this. There's three of you and only one of me. So simply on mathematic grounds, you're the priority. Now let me pack my stuff so I can disappear before they come for me tomorrow."

The men look at each other and smile.

"See, that's why we want you to stay," James says, his eyes turning soft. "Please, stay. For us."

"I can't." I shake my head. "As much as I would love to be human, I'm not. And I won't become one overnight by marrying one of you. Maybe on paper, yes, but look at me! Look at the metal on my body, look at the camera in my skull. I'm not human and I'll never be. I'm a hybrid and that won't change just because you three want it to."

All of them look sad, just like I feel. I've always wanted to be human, but I've also been rational enough from the start to know that it's impossible. My mind tells me that it's a waste of time to hunger for something that will never be, but my heart ignores it. My heart, my human heart. It's not metal, no, it's flesh and blood. And I bet it could fall in love, if I let it.

But I won't. Not even with these three men, my masters, who are willing to give up so much for me. No.

It would be so easy, my silly little heart whispers. Just let go of your fears and stay.

But I can't. One day they'll meet a real woman they'll like and I'll be in their way. I couldn't do that to them. They've been kind to me all my life, they've even paid me a wage which is unheard of for hybrids, so I cannot let them destroy their own lives.

Marrying would be a mistake. Logic clearly says that.

"I'm leaving," I mumble, my voice not quite functioning the way I want it to. Even my vocal cords are now against me. So is my whole body. I can't get myself to move away from the men in front of me.

"Don't," Dan says softly. "Please, don't."

"But..."

"Can I prove it to you?" he asks and gets up, stopping close in front of me until I can feel his warm breath on my face.

"Prove what?"

"That marrying us will be worth it."

I frown, unsure of what he's talking about.

"Yes?"

Instead of an answer, he cups my face and pulls me closer. His lips touch mine, so soft, so gentle, and I instinctively open my mouth. I've never been kissed before; who would want to kiss a hybrid?!

But Dan is doing just that. His lips move on mine and I'm not quite sure what to do, so I copy what he does. Something touches my lower lip, his tongue. More warmth, more softness. He seems to wait for my reaction, but when I don't protest, he enters my mouth with that very same tongue, doing things to my heart that nobody else has ever done. He's all I can think of, all I can focus on, his touch, his lips, his breath. How am I supposed to think like that? How am I supposed to resist?

I suck in a deep breath and he ends the kiss, looking at me in worry.

"I'm sorry, I..." he says apologetically.

I curse myself for making him think that I didn't like it.

"I think you were close to proving it," I whisper with a smile. I have no idea where I take the confidence from. "But you may have to do some more proving."

CHAPTER 4

I can't believe I'm doing this. It's crazy.

I'm wearing a long white skirt that's ruffled up at the back, a dark red corset with a white blouse underneath, and a white fur cape that Dan put over my shoulders because he thought I was cold. No, I'm not cold. I'm excited and scared and worried and out of my mind.

Hybrids don't get married. We don't have partners. We don't do things like that.

This is like a dream but I'm not quite sure yet if it's a good one. I want it to be, so much. I want this to be the best day of my life, like they say in the books. But I can't get the thought out of my head that I'm destroying my masters' lives.

I suppose I can't call them my masters anymore. My husbands. My men.

All three of them are waiting nervously, fumbling with their suits. James has a pocket watch that he keeps flipping open before closing it again. We're waiting for the priest who will wed us.

I've never been so tense in all my life.

Finally, the sound of the heavy door knocker signals that it's time. The priest has arrived. Oh my, what am I doing?!

While Dan goes downstairs to welcome Father Murray, Luke wanders around the room, checking everything is in place. They've lit candles and got some flowers from the kitchen where I'd put them in a large vase just yesterday. Now they're dotted all around the living room, adding some colour to the dark walls. The chandelier is brightly lit and so is the fireplace. It's a cosy atmosphere, not too serious.

I don't think I could cope with a proper ceremony right now. My head is telling me to run away still, while my heart is too excited to beat properly.

James approaches me from behind.

"Close your eyes," he whispers softly and I do so without thinking.

Something cold touches my throat, something metal. Automatically, I lift a hand to feel what's happening, and meet with James's warm fingers. Hot and cold at the same time. Something like excitement is bubbling up in me. It's the same feeling I had earlier when Dan kissed me. It's new and strange but very pleasant.

"This belonged to our mother," he says and I can hear that he's smiling. He fumbles with the necklace clasp before stepping back, gently turning me around. His dark eyes are fixed on my throat before wandering up to take in my face.

"Beautiful. It suits you."

I explore the necklace with my fingers. It's a thin chain with a large, heavy pendant. The metal is quickly taking on my skin's temperature and I almost miss the coolness of it. I remember the mirror above the fireplace and go to see what James just gave me.

It's stunning. The pendant is made up of a large amber in the centre, surrounded by dozens of tiny copper and iron cogs.

"Our father brought home the cogs from the factory he worked in," James explains. "He wasn't allowed to, of course, but mother had always loved that kind of things. He never told us where he got the jewel from. Anyway, she told us to pass it on to the first wife one of the three of us would marry. I think she would have laughed if she knew that all three of us are marrying you, in a way."

I'm having trouble fighting back the tears. He's so convinced that this is the right decision. He really wants to marry me. Does resisting make me a bad person?

"We don't have a ring, so this will need to do as the promise that we'll get you one as soon as possible," Luke explains, joining James in looking at me in admiration.

"It suits you," Dan says and only now do I notice that he's come back upstairs, Father Murray in tow. He's an older gentleman with a flurry of grey hair escaping from beneath his black top hat. His long coat has seen better days, but that's nothing special here in the city. He's smiling at me, which is the most important thing.

"So you are the lucky girl?" He extends a hand and I cautiously take it. Most humans would never shake hands with a hybrid. I've not met the priest before, even though he's the masters' godfather. If he's visited before, it must have been while I was running errands.

"Father." I do a courtesy like I've seen other women do it, human women, but I fail miserably. I'm not good at being elegant, I shouldn't even have tried.

"I've told him what's going on," Dan explains and Father Murray nods.

"Who of you three will be the lucky gentleman?"

My masters - fiancées? - look at each other questioningly.

"We could go with the oldest," James says hesitantly. "That would be Dan."

"Let's play dice. Whoever rolls the highest number will be the bridegroom," Dan suggests and produces three dice from his pockets. He must have been planning this.

He gives one each to his brothers and they go over to the low coffee table to play. Luke is first, he rolls a five. James gets a two, Dan another five. My heart is pounding in my chest. Strangely enough, I don't mind who of them will win. I know they'll all be equal in the relationship, and somehow, that doesn't bother me.

"And again," James chuckles, stepping back from the table. Luke spins the die in his fingers before throwing it. Three. Now it's Dan's turn. I hold my breath. Six.

"Congratulations, brother," Luke says and shakes Dan's hand. He smiles happily though; he doesn't seem to mind. Neither does James.

The priest opens the book he has with him. Parish Registry, it says on the front in large golden letters.

Dan and I take our places in front of the fireplace, which is doubling as a church's altar. James stands on Dan's right while Luke is on my left.

"What shall I call you, Miss?" he asks me, pulling out a fountain pen.

"Dex."

"Just Dex?"

"Yes, just Dex." I smile at Dan who winks at me in return. It started out as his nickname for me, but now it's turned into a real name.

"Miss Dex marrying Mr Daniel Walker..." Father Murray mutters to himself as he fills in an empty page in his book.

He looks up at Dan, giving him a stern look that almost passes as paternal.

"Will you love her, comfort her, honour and keep her, in sickness and in health? And forsaking all others, keep only to her as long as you both shall live?"

"I will," Dan answers solemnly and my heart does another flutter. Is this really happening?

The priest turns to me. "Will you obey him and serve him, love, honour and keep him, in sickness and in health? And forsaking all others, keep only to these three men as long as you all shall live?"

I startle at the obey and serve bit, but I assume that's the standard vow for all women.

"I will," I answer, my voice hitching only slightly.

Dan takes my hands in his, looking me straight into the eyes.

"I thee wed: with my body I thee worship, and with all my worldly goods, I thee endow."

His eyes are soft and beautiful. For the first time, I'm starting to believe that this is real. That they really want it. That we're going to be husbands and wife.

"I thee wed: with my body I thee worship, and with all

my worldly goods, I thee endow," Luke whispers on my left, and James does the same.

Dan looks as if he's going to say something, but suddenly, there are three loud knocks on the door downstairs.

Panic spreads through me and I rip my hands out of Dan's.

"They're here for me," I croak. "I should have run."

The priest pushes a pen into my hand. "Quick, sign here."

He points at a line at the bottom of the marriage certificate. I quickly write my name on there; I've never had to sign anything before. I've not had time to practice a pretty signature.

Dan does an elegant flourish on the groom's line, signing away his life to me. We're married now. On paper. For real.

I'm married to a human.

Oh Lord.

They knock again, louder this time.

"I'll go," Father Murray says and leaves the room to go downstairs. I look at my men, my husbands. They seem less scared than I am, but still worried.

Dex Walker. I try out the name, first in my mind, then with my lips. "Dex Walker."

I smile. I am Dex Walker and I'm going to show them that I'm no longer just a hybrid. I am a woman married to three men, three human men. They can kiss my corset and disappear to where they came from.

I rush out of the room and down the stairs where the priest is talking animatedly with two large men. They don't look impressed by what he's saying. He's waving his registry book in their faces, but they may not even be able to read, let alone understand what it means.

I squeeze past him until I'm standing right in front of them.

"Gentlemen, what's the matter?"

They stare at me as if I've grown a second head.

"You're to come with us," one of them finally growls, his voice that of someone smoking and drinking far too much.

"What did he tell you to do, exactly?" I ask them and they look at each other in confusion.

"Bring the hybrid," the second one says and I nod patiently.

"Well, what Father Murray here is trying to tell you is that there is no hybrid at this address."

The first man's eyes are bulging now. "But you're a hybrid."

I smile. "Not any longer. You see, I am married now. To a human. Which means that you can't take me with you. Go back and tell your master that he can speak to my husband's lawyer, if he still wants me."

Again, they look at each other, hoping that one of them might know what to do. Eventually, they make the right choice and leave, grumbling and threatening.

When they're gone, I breathe in deeply. Showing such confidence wasn't easy.

"Now I know why they're so keen to keep you," Father Murray says kindly. "I better leave and tell their lawyer to make arrangements. In the meantime, the four of you should enjoy your honeymoon."

I look at him in confusion. "What's that?"

He chuckles. "The time when husband and wife get to

know each other further. Have some fun with them, you deserve it."

With that, he leaves.

He's telling me to have fun with my husbands? Well, guess what I'm going to do.

Exactly that.

CHAPTER 5

SEVERAL MONTHS LATER...

I never thought the sky was this blue. I was always under the impression that it was grey, maybe a slight bluish tinge, but nothing like this bright, pale blue that seems to be crashing down on us. There's no smog to keep the sky separated from the endless fields we're travelling through.

It's the first time I've been out of the city. Or maybe I have, but if that's the case, then it was before I was made a hybrid and I can't remember that part of my life.

"Isn't it beautiful?" Dan asks, wrapping an arm around my shoulders as he peers through the dusty window of the carriage.

I can only nod. It's so surreal to be here in this beautiful place. No buildings as far as the eye can see, only fields, blue sky, fresh air. Luke has opened the window in the roof of the carriage, letting in the sweet smell of the countryside. I can't place the scent. There's none of the smoke and dirt of the city, none of the decay and rot in the Lower Zones, none of the opium sometimes wafting through the streets at night. The air here smells like something, but I can't identify what it is. I'm not sure my husbands can, either. It's been years since they last left the city.

Even now, Luke is looking a little pale and Andrew is still coughing every few minutes. There's a reason they never leave the house. For them to do it now, for me, means more than they can imagine.

"It looks like it might snow soon," Dan says, pointing at a few scattered clouds on the horizon.

I turn to him, taking my eyes off the sky for the first time in at least an hour.

"How do you know?"

"It smells like snow and you see how those clouds are torn in places? Our grandma always said that if the clouds look like bedspreads being shaken and crumpled, then it's going to snow."

"It smells like snow?" I repeat. "What does snow smell like?"

Dan grins. "Like this. Breathe it in, Dex. Feel the moisture in the air. Feel how it coats your lungs, how it drives out all the dirt of the city."

I close my eyes, wondering if what I'm smelling is the scent of snow. Of course, it snows in the city, but it immediately turns into a grey sludge that stinks like everything else. It's only pure and white for the few seconds before it touches the ground. Here, it will be different, I'm sure.

"Is it much further?" I ask, opening my eyes and

staring at the dirt road making its way through fields and barren lands. The crops were harvested months ago, so now all that remains are weeds. It should look sad and depressing, but all I can see is the hope of new plants making these fields their home in the spring. Despite everything being so brown, there are shades of green as well, so much more green than I'm used to. I think if I could, I'd live in the countryside rather than the city. But of course, that's not my choice.

"No, we're almost there," Andrew replies, his voice hoarse from all the coughing. "See that hill in the distance? The farm is just beyond it."

"I can't wait," I tell him with a smile. "It sounds so beautiful."

"We should have taken you there before. The journey by itself is worth it, and getting out of the city even more so. And the food..." He grins. "Aunt Laura has the best cook ever."

"Bread and butter pudding," Dan sighs. "Treacle tarts. Trifle."

I've not had any of those things before, but the way he says them, they sound delicious. My husbands aren't poor, but they're also not rich enough to be able to afford the ingredients needed for some treats. Sugar is one of the most expensive goods there is, almost as pricey as opium. Sweets are a rarity, but they've told me that their aunt is so wealthy that she even puts sugar in her tea. It seems like a waste when you can use honey instead.

"She'll fatten us up," Andrew predicts. "She thinks everyone should be round and large, especially men. She's never accepted that our illness means we can't put on as much weight as other people."

"I like you how you are," I say with a shrug. "You wouldn't all fit into the bed if you were any bigger."

They all laugh.

"I love the way you think," Dan mutters and pulls me closer until I'm almost on his lap. "I just hope Aunt Laura got the hint and has put us all in the same room."

The hill is getting ever closer and tingles of nervousness spread in my chest. This will be the first time I'm meeting my husbands' family. Neither of their parents is still alive, but they do have an assortment of aunts and uncles, cousins and even two nieces. They're not close with a lot of them, but Aunt Laura is one of the exceptions. Let's hope she'll like me.

* * *

"Why did you bring your hybrid?"

The words slam into me like a punch and I feel sick.

Andrew puts an arm around my shoulders, pulling me against him. I think it's supposed to be both for reassurance and to show his aunt who I am.

Aunt Laura is staring at us, her cheeks red, almost matching her bright auburn hair that's braided in an elaborate style. It's likely taken hours for it to look that way. She's wearing a black dress with a high collar, decorated with tiny black pearls. On the way, my men told me she's been wearing black ever since her husband died five years ago. She's rather large; her bosom is straining against the delicate fabric and her bum is absolutely enormous.

"You don't need a servant here, I've got my own."

I'm sure she's intelligent enough to understand that

I'm not their servant, but her stoic expression predicts that she's not going to simply smile and accept the fact that I'm not human.

"Aunt Laura, meet our wife, Dex."

Luke's smiling, but there's steel in his voice.

"That has to be a joke." She's still staring at me in disapproval. I resist the urge to look down at myself and check whether my corset and skirt are flawless and without stains. We've been travelling for most of the day, so a few wrinkles in my clothes should be acceptable.

Luke takes his place on my left and takes my hand.

"Dex is our wife and you will respect her as such."

Aunt Laura frowns, the wrinkles on her face growing deeper.

"But she's a hybrid! She's a machine!"

I flinch. That's about the worst thing she could have said. I may have steel parts in me, but I feel human and she's not going to take that away from me with her poisonous words.

I step forward, leaving my men behind.

"I am not a machine," I say coldly, looking her straight in the eyes. I know my mechanical eye will not help convince her, but it's not like I can simply remove it. It's part of me, an implant that's fused with my face just like my metal arm and the metal plates in my legs. I'm a hybrid, part human, part metal, but I'm *not* a machine. I'm alive.

"I am the wife of your nephews and we've come here to spend our honeymoon together. If you have a problem with that, we're going to move on and find somewhere else to stay. We don't need your approval and neither do I need to listen to your insults."

She keeps eye contact, her eyes just as piercing as I hope mine are. We stare at each other, neither of us backing down. She's a strong woman, that much is clear, but so am I.

I might not be one hundred per cent human, but in my mind, I am. I won't be bullied.

"Aunt Laura," Dan begins from behind me but she shuts him up with a wave of her hand.

"Don't, this is between her and me." Her frown lessens a little. "Tell me, hybrid, do you love them?"

I don't hesitate to reply. "Yes."

"Is your heart human or metal?"

That question surprises me. Nobody has ever asked me that before.

"I'm not sure," I reply truthfully. "But I can love, so I assume it's human."

"How can you not know?" she asks, confusion mirroring in her eyes.

"I only know about the modifications that I can see. There are scars on my body, so I assume that they've implanted parts within me, but there's no record of what they did to me during the conversion, and all I remember is the pain."

"Pain?" she asks, her expression softening. "You can feel pain?"

I look at her incredulously. "Of course I do. I'm not a machine. I don't remember who I was before the conversion, so the first memory I have is pain."

I've never told my men that and I don't know why I'm saying it now. This woman doesn't need to know. None of them do. It's private.

Finally, she breaks eye contact and looks at the

ground. I'm not sure how to interpret her expression. Is it shame? Confusion?

"Welcome to my home," she says quietly. "Come on in."

She turns and disappears in the large house, leaving me and my men standing outside.

"We're going to talk about this later," Dan announces tonelessly. I don't turn around to look at him. I'm scared of what they might think of me now. I should never have said what I said. There's a reason hybrids are different from humans.

CHAPTER 6

The house is even bigger inside than it looks from the outside. It's also old, very old. Aunt Laura's family has lived here for generations and I can almost feel all the ghosts of her ancestors walking through the corridors.

There are cracks in some of the walls and a few of the rooms are locked, probably because it's too much effort to keep them clean and tidy. Aunt Laura lives here on her own, now that all her children have moved out, and the house is far too big for one person, even with her servants and the cook.

While the men are bringing in our trunks, I look around. I've never been in such a big house before. In the city, everything is much smaller as space is scarce. Even Mr Bradley, the richest man I know, has a smaller mansion than this farmhouse. Either Aunt Laura is incredibly rich, or things are simply different in the countryside.

There's a beautiful cast iron bathtub in one of the

bathrooms and I make a mental note to take a bath there later on. White candle stubs are stuck to the edges of the tub, signs Aunt Laura must enjoy a relaxing bath here from time to time as well.

The next room I enter is a massive kitchen, currently filled with steam and the smell of fresh bread.

"Are you new?" a male voice asks from somewhere beyond the steam. It takes a moment for me to be able to see him. He's a large bald man wearing a stained apron.

"New?" I ask in confusion.

"A new servant," he says impatiently. "Did the Lady's nephews bring you along? We don't have hybrids here, but I guess we'll take what we get."

"I'm not a servant," I mutter, unwilling to get into another argument. I turn and leave as fast as I can, ignoring the man's shouts.

I no longer feel like exploring. Instead, I head towards the sitting room I saw when entering the house. Aunt Laura is waiting there for me, sitting on an armchair in a way that makes me think of a queen on her throne. A fire is burning brightly in the fireplace behind her, filling the room with a soft, warm light. It's about three times as big as our fireplace back home. It must cost a fortune to get enough wood and coal, but by now, I doubt cost is an issue for my husbands' aunt.

"Sit down," she tells me and points at another armchair opposite hers. I do as she asks, still a little hesitant to be in a room alone with her. Even though I seem to have won our earlier argument, I'm still wary of this woman. She's formidable and I'm not sure she's accepted me yet. Maybe she's simply waited until I'm without my men so she can spit her poison without witnesses.

She takes a beautiful ornate teapot from the small side table to her right and pours us a cup each. The tea is a lovely shade of brown, not like the muddy looking tea we have at home. Maybe it's the water that's cleaner here or the quality of the tea.

When she hands me my cup – placed on a saucer so thin I'm worried simply touching it might break it – I notice her rings. Each finger is adorned with at least two rings, all of them gold.

"Those are pretty," I say to break the silence.

"Heirlooms," she replies with a shrug as if she's not wearing a small fortune on her fingers. "I don't like leaving my jewellery unattended."

For some strange reason, that makes me sad. Is she so scared of thieves that she feels like she needs to wear dozens of rings at the same time? It seems like a lonely thing to do.

"How did you meet my nephews?" she asks, leaning back in her chair, her cup balanced perfectly between her thumb and her index finger. She's even got her pinkie straight and extended, just like I've seen posh women do it at Mr Bradley's house.

"I was a gift to them from one of their business associates." I don't expand on that, I don't want to dwell on the fact that I was passed on from one person to another like a commodity.

She nods and takes a sip of tea. "Was it love at first sight?"

"Not for me." I think back to the moment I first saw them. I was confused, freshly converted and not used to my new body yet. My mechanical eye was playing havoc with my brain and there was a deep ache in my bones that just wouldn't go away. I didn't listen to most of what was said and was grateful when they showed me the attic where I was going to sleep. It even had a latch so I could lock myself in at night. Back then, I thought it was an oversight on the men's behalf, but now I'm sure it was intentional, a sign of their kindness. They never saw me as a machine like so many others. For them, I was a person right from the start.

"And for them?" she asks, ripping me from my memories.

I shrug. "You'll have to ask them."

She raises a perfectly manicured eyebrow. "You've never talked about it?"

"No."

I don't tell her that the men have tried, but I've changed the topic every time. I'm afraid of what they might say. I don't want to hear that I was always just a servant to them. I don't want to imagine how they felt about me at the beginning. I prefer to focus on how our relationship is now. Three men, one woman, nothing else matters.

"My husband hated me when we first met," she says suddenly, surprising me. "He didn't want to marry me, but his parents had forced him. He was in love with a girl from the village, far too lowly for his position, but he didn't care about that. He was always a bit of a rebel." She smiles and for the first time, I see the kind and friendly aunt my men told me about. "He was absent for most of the first few years of our marriage. I think he slept with most of the women in the village just to spite his parents.

When he was home, he didn't talk to me. At night, we slept in separate rooms. He never even touched me..."

Her voice trails off and her eyes have taken on a strange shimmer.

"That must have been hard," I say gently, confused why she's telling me all this. It seems very private.

"It was. It made me ill. I think I was suffering from a broken heart. I'd read all those stories of love and princes and heroes worshipping their ladies, so to have the exact opposite in my life broke me. I fell into a sort of dream state, unable and unwilling to interact with the world. That was the moment my husband decided to change."

She smiles and takes another sip of tea, reminding me that my own drink is getting cold.

"He cared for me, started talking to me, turned into the husband I'd always dreamed of. He stopped seeing other women and when I got better, he joined me in my bed. We had four children, one after the other, all of them perfect and beautiful."

Once again, she falls silent, staring into her cup.

"Why are you telling me this?" I ask quietly.

She laughs softly. "I don't even know myself. I've not told anyone this in a long time."

"I've never told anyone about the pain of conversion. Maybe we're even now. We've both told each other secrets."

"That we have. Maybe I wanted to apologise for how I behaved earlier. It's not your fault you're not human."

Even though it's true, it still stings. I don't like being reminded that I'm different.

"It's not your fault you're not a hybrid," I reply drily and she chuckles.

"Good point. How about some cake?"

I nod and she rings a little bronze bell, waiting for one of the servants to come. Instead, the door opens and my husbands enter.

"Are we interrupting something?" James asks with a smile. "Girl talk?"

"I will have you know that I'm a lady," his aunt says and points at the sofas on the other side of the room, inviting them to sit. "And your wife isn't exactly a girl either."

I expect another barb at me not being human, but instead, she says, "She's a lady, too."

Dan chuckles. "That she is. Lady Walker does have a nice ring to it."

"I prefer Dex," I mutter, but they're not listening.

"Lady Dex might be prettier than Lady Walker," James argues.

"How about Lady Dex Walker?" Luke suggests with a wide grin. "Or Lady Luke Walker?"

I groan. "Stop it. I'm not a lady and I never will be."

Luckily, we're interrupted by one of the servants responding the Aunt Laura's bell. While the maid runs off to get us some cake, I keep having to fight the impulse to join her in running errands. I'm not used to being the one to sit and be waited on. Of course, the men no longer treat me as their servant, but I don't know anything else, I've always been inferior to others. I'm not sure I'll ever get used to not being at the bottom of the food chain, but somewhere in between.

CHAPTER 7

*T*he men were right. It really did smell like snow during our coach journey yesterday. Now, the ground is covered in at least an inch of pure white snow, untouched by anyone, least of all smog and dirt.

"How can it be so white?" I ask, more to myself than to the men. They're still in bed in various stages of sleepiness. They pushed together two double beds to make space of us all. At home, we sometimes all sleep in one bed, and sometimes I share a bed with only one of them. While they're all happy to share, they also like to have me to themselves from time to time. Even though we've only been married for a few months now, we've already established something of a routine.

"I'm going outside," I announce and slip out of the room before anyone can protest.

"Put on a coat!" Andrew shouts but I'm already running down the creaky stairs and out of the front door. I only notice that I forgot to put on my shoes when I step into the snow. My feet are as human as they get and while

I don't feel the cold as much as real humans, it's still a bit of a shock to my senses. I wiggle my toes and begin to walk through the snow, leaving a barely visible trail of footsteps behind. The sun is barely reaching above the crest of the hill towering above the house, but the snow is making everything seem much brighter than it really is.

My feet are getting cold, so I sit down in the snow instead, running my hands over the tiny ice crystals that have formed on the surface. Of course, only my left hand feels the cold, the right one is metal, already cold and lifeless.

My white nightgown is wet, the snow seeping into the fabric as water, but I stay where I am, simply enjoying the sensation of being in the clean, fresh air. A bit of cold isn't going to stop me from sitting out here. Who knows when I'm next going to experience snow like this? No, I'm going to stay outside all day, savouring every second.

I lie back and stretch out my arms and legs, moving them through the snow, making small snow hills on either side of me. From above, it must look like I've drawn myself wings into the snow.

A few isolated snowflakes are still spilling from the dark clouds above, landing gently on my face. One of them touches my lips, immediately turning into a drop of water. I stick out my tongue and close my eyes, waiting for the next snowflake to land on there. When it does, it tickles in the most delightful way.

"Having fun?"

It's Andrew. I don't open my eyes but I smile when a blanket is gently put on top of me. It doesn't stop the cold seeping into my body from beneath, but it's a beautiful gesture that makes me want to kiss him. For that though,

I'd have to sit up, but I'm busy waiting for snowflakes to land on my tongue.

"You're adorable," he chuckles and sits down by my side. "Can I be your snowflake?"

I open my eyes and look up just in time to see him bend down until his lips meet my tongue. He tastes and feels even better than the snow.

I let him wrap his arms around me and lift me until I'm in his embrace, our mouths entwined in a dance of lips and tongues and sparks racing all the way through my body. I snuggle against his warm chest, running my hands over his back. He's wearing a thick coat but I wish he wasn't. I want to feel more of him. Yes, I was with my men last night, but I felt a bit self-conscious, being in someone else's house and bed, so we left it at a few kisses and touches. Now though, I want more.

Never stopping our kiss, I unbutton his coat and slide my hands underneath it.

"Here? Outside?" he whispers against my lips and I smile.

"Yes. In the snow."

* * *

When we return to the house, the sun has risen fully and is making the snow sparkle like diamonds. Andrew has wrapped me in the blanket and has put the coat on top of it, making me look three times the size I am. He didn't listen to my protests, and to be honest, I'm glad. I'm cold and maybe it's a good idea to go inside.

Breakfast awaits us in the dining room. Dan and Luke

are already sitting there, Aunt Laura at the end of the long table, once again looking like royalty.

There's fresh bread and delicate pastries, homemade jam and butter that looks like it might actually not be rancid. This is going to be a feast and it's only breakfast.

"Why do you look like you slept outside?" Aunt Laura asks, raising an eyebrow.

Andrew grins. "We looked at the snow."

"For two hours?"

He shrugs. "There was a lot of snow to look at."

Aunt Laura turns to me. "You should get changed, dear, or you'll get a cold."

"I don't get ill," I say automatically, but my teeth are chattering, mocking my words.

"Change. Now." Dan commands and I can't help but do as he says. When he talks in that bossy voice, I don't really have a choice. I'd do whatever he wanted if he speaks in that way. It's got some kind of power over me, and I love it.

I run back to our bedroom and swiftly change into a dress. I run a brush through my tousled hair, but give up pretty quickly, deciding I'll try and get my hair under control after breakfast. Our little snow adventure has been exhausting and I'm starving.

I open the door and almost run into a large man. The cook from yesterday. He's staring at me with disgust.

"You're a hybrid," he growls without preamble.

"Well spotted." I don't even try to hide the sarcasm.

"And you're married to one of the Lady's nephews."

"Right again."

He takes a step forward and I immediately walk back into the bedroom.

"That's disgusting." Without warning, he spits, warm saliva hitting my cheek. I flinch, further retreating away from him.

He follows, seemingly enjoying my fear.

"Things like you shouldn't even exist." His voice is full of revulsion that makes me shiver. This man is a threat and I really need to get away from him. "Maybe I should rid the world of you. The men won't miss you, I'm sure you're just their plaything. Do you have metal between your legs? I wonder if that feels good."

"I'm their wife," I bite out, resisting the urge to cower from him. "They love me."

He laughs. "They might love your metal pussy, but rest assured, they don't love the rest of you. No human could ever love a hybrid. You're nothing but a machine, an abomination that's only good to serve."

"I'm not a machine," I hiss and try to run. Despite his bulk, he's faster than I thought and grabs me just when I reach the door.

"Not so fast. I want to find out why they keep you first. Then, I'm going to see where you have your off switch."

He pushes me against the wall, his hands gripping my upper arms so hard that I'm sure I'm going to get bruises. I struggle against him and try to knee him in the balls, but he's got one leg pressed against mine, making it impossible for me to move. He's far too large and strong. I wish they'd equipped me with some kind of defence mechanism, but all I have are a few metal parts, an arm that can be used as a hidden cache and an eye that I can't see with. Thank you, creators, really helpful.

"Help!" I scream, deciding it's time to get others involved. "He-!"

The cook lets go of one of my arms to put his hand on my mouth. Luckily, it's the right arm that's now free, the metal one. I gather my strength and hit him on the neck as hard as I can. He screams and funnily enough, his scream is louder than my own just moments earlier. There are voices and noises down below, the sound of chairs being pushed back, then footsteps on the creaky stairs. They've heard us.

The man seems to realise the same thing and lets go of me.

"If you don't leave this house, I'll disassemble you," he hisses and steps back. "We don't want your kind here."

The door bangs open and my husbands storm into the room, followed by Aunt Laura.

"What's going on?" Dan shouts, stepping between the cook and me. "What did you do?"

The fury in his voice makes me shiver slightly. None of my men are violent people, but right now, all three of them look like they're about to launch themselves at the cook.

"Nothing," he mutters. "We just had a little chat."

Dan turns to me, inspecting me from top to bottom.

"Are you alright?" he asks sharply. I rub my arms where the cook grabbed me. I'm going to have bruises tonight.

I'm not sure what to say. No, I'm not alright, but I also don't want to start some big drama. I don't think the cook is going to do anything to me now that I know of the threat. I'm going to stick with my men and stay out of the servants' way.

But then, why should I change my behaviour because

of this bully? I should be able to walk around on my own without fear that he might attack me again.

"He threatened me," I tell them, surprised by the slight tremor in my voice. "He wants to kill me."

Aunt Laura gasps. "Mr Brown? Is that true?"

The cook turns to her. "She's an abomination," he growls. "She's a threat to you and this house, my Lady. I only mean to keep us safe."

Her eyes turn to ice as she glares at him. "How dare you! Dex is my guest and the wife of my nephews. She is welcome here. You, however, are not. Pack your bags, you're fired."

He frowns, confused. "But my Lady, I'm-"

"Leave. Now," she says coldly. "I'd rather cook lunch myself than have you stay in this house."

He seems to want to say something but then turns, not without giving me a stare that speaks of pain and torture. And death, most likely. I'm not scared of him, though. I've dealt with bullies who despise hybrids all my life. This isn't the first time I've been assaulted, although it might be the first time my men saw it.

"Are you alright?" Dan repeats as soon as the cook and Aunt Laura have left the room.

I step into his arms and let myself be held.

"I am now," I whisper as the other two join our hug, surrounding me with their warmth.

CHAPTER 8

The first time I had sex with my husbands, I was ashamed of my scars. Before then, they'd never seen me naked. Never seen the scars crisscrossing my body. Even though I can't remember a time without those thick pink lines all over my skin, I still feel shame for having them.

My men never even blinked an eye. Well, Dan's expression turned into fire and ice, fury for the people who did this to me, but he never told me that they were ugly. They all accept them, more than I can myself take them for what they are. Part of me.

"Take off your clothes," Andrew whispers huskily while James closes the door, keeping any prying eyes outside. After the encounter with the cook, I'm glad the three of them are here with me. I want to be held and cherished and told that I'm everything to them. I want to forget what that man said about hybrids. I want to feel human as they take me, as they give me the pleasure I never thought possible.

I undress very slowly while the three of them watch me. I know I'm teasing them, but I enjoy their heated gazes and the growing bulges against their trousers. Dan helps me with unlacing my corset, but then steps back to watch the show. When I'm only in my underwear, I hesitate for a moment, aware of the scars that are no longer hidden beneath several layers of fabric.

"Continue," Andrew encourages me and I look up, locking eyes with him. There's so much love in those eyes, so much emotion, that I feel safe enough to pull my camisole over my head and let it slip to the floor. Now the only thing left are my drawers. They're shorter than I'm used to, going till just above my knee. It's the latest fashion and a treat from James. He likes to buy me clothes.

"If you don't hurry up, I'm going to rip them off your body," Dan groans. He's opened his trousers and is stroking himself as he watches me with greedy eyes.

"Do it," I challenge him and in seconds, he's kneeling in front of me, pulling down my drawers, helping me step out of them. He stands up and looks at me for a moment, then puts his hands on my hips and pulls me closer.

"You're beautiful, Dex," he whispers hoarsely and leans down a little, taking my left nipple in his mouth. He uses his hands to gently squeeze the other one, running circles around my puckered areola. I moan and arch my back, confident that he won't let me fall. My skin is hot and I am desperate for him to touch me in other places. He's teasing me, but I need more. I grip his head with both hands, pulling him off my breast and pushing him downwards.

He chuckles and lets me guide him between my legs.

When his tongue touches me there, right where I want him, I almost fall apart. His tongue is a wicked instrument of lust, moving in circles just fast enough to drive me crazy.

He flicks his tongue over my bud one more time before entering me with it, sucking hard and swallowing my wetness. I put my hands on his head, both to guide him to my sweet spot and to steady myself. I'm a mess, moaning and quivering, and then screaming when he makes me come. That was too fast, too quick, but I can't help it. My knees buckle but the other two have seen my predicament and then I'm in Andrew's arms as he carries me over to the bed. He gently lays me down and spreads my legs, then kneels on the floor, looking right where Dan's tongue was a moment ago. I must be glistening with wetness.

James lies down on the bed beside me and takes one of my nipples into his mouth, sucking hard. I gasp and arch my back at the same time as Andrew enters me with a finger. He glides in easily and adds a second one. I groan in protest. I want more than his fingers. I never get to complain though, because Dan has moved onto my other side and silences me with a kiss. His lips are hot and soft. I can taste myself on them, and on his tongue when I open my mouth to let him in. He kisses me passionately, but I have to force myself to respond in kind because my senses are overflowing with being touched by three men at once. James is massaging my breasts, his fingers twirling my nipples, while his tongue is drawing lines across my belly.

Andrew removes his fingers from me and before I even realise what's happening, he fills me with his hardness, stretching me with that strange sensation between pain and ecstasy. I moan against Dan's mouth and he gently nips my bottom lip in response. I love when he does that.

I spread my legs further and push my pelvis forward, giving Andrew even better access. He takes full advantage of it, thrusting into me with new vigour. Dan's kiss is keeping me from making all the noises I'd like to make, but occasionally, a moan slips out, especially when James starts suckling on my nipples.

I close my eyes and let myself drift, thinking of nothing but the pleasure my husbands are giving me. One orgasm blurs into another as Andrew comes inside of me with a loud groan, his place quickly taken by James. Hands run over my breasts, lips brush over my skin, and at some point, I start stroking someone's erection, eliciting sounds that only make me grip him tighter.

We're a mess of sounds and touches, all connected by our shared love for each other. I wrap my legs around the man who's still pushing into me, who's filling me up completely. We're teetering on the edge, but I can't bring myself to let us jump into bliss. That will mean this moment is over and they'll stop touching me. I'm not going to let him go. I'm not going to let *any* of them go. They're mine, my husbands, my men, and I am their wife, hybrid or not.

CHAPTER 9

My husbands look better than ever. Their skin is flushed in a healthy rose shade rather than their usual pallor. They don't cough as much and they seem happier here in the countryside. They're not as stressed, either. I've never been so relaxed as I am here, and it's just the same for them.

We've extended our honeymoon by two weeks to spend Christmas with Aunt Laura. I think she enjoys the company as well. None of her own children will be able to come here for the festivities, so it saves her from having to travel to them or be here on her own.

I've really come to like her. Of course, I've not forgotten her earlier hostility, but I'm now convinced that was just due to her being worried for her nephews. Maybe she saw me as someone taking advantage of them. Maybe she would have even been the same to a human woman.

"Darling, would you pass me the tea?"

I smile and pour a cup, handing it back to Aunt Laura.

She's throning in her armchair as always, but instead of her usual knitting, today her lap is covered in wrapping paper. I've been helping wrap presents for her relatives, all the while worrying that I don't have anything to give to her and my husbands. I had planned to get them something once we were back in the city, but now that we're staying here, there's no way for me to buy them something. There are no shops near the farmhouse, and I've been told that taking the carriage to the nearest village would be too dangerous on my own. Hybrids are rare here and Mr Brown's attitude is widespread among the locals. Aunt Laura's had a bit of a cough in the past week, otherwise she would have come with me. So here I am, stuck, resigned to having nothing but my love as a present for my men.

"Only one more to go," Aunt Laura says with a smile, putting yet another beautifully wrapped present on the pile next to her. "Then we can move on to yours."

I look at the floor. "I don't have any yet."

She grins and points at a chest in the corner. "Surprise!"

I frown, confused. That chest is always there, but I've never opened it. With a shrug, I get up and kneel down in front of it. The mahogany wood is beautifully polished, making it shimmer in the light of the fireplace. Inside is an assortment of items, all of them familiar.

"I found your list," Aunt Laura says softly. "I hope you don't mind I had one of the servants buy them for you."

I jump to my feet, run towards her and give her a hug.

I'd forgotten the list I'd written with the things I'd give to my men if I could. Most of them were just dreams, items I could never afford. A new pocket watch for Luke.

A chess set for Dan because a few of his chess pieces have gone missing and he wants them all to match. For Andrew, an illustrated copy of Homer's Iliad.

"It's nothing," the old woman chuckles while I can't stop blubbering my thanks. "I'm glad the boys are getting what they actually want. I would never have known what to give them. You did me a favour, darling."

"Thank you," I say for about the hundredth time. "You don't even know how much this means to me."

She pats my back. "It's lovely having young people in the house again. It's been quiet here for far too long."

"I'm trying to persuade them that we should stay a little longer," I admit, finally letting her go from my overenthusiastic hug. "Their business seems to be going well while their assistant is looking after everything. They don't need to be in the city, they can keep their eye on it from here."

"I agree, it's good for them. They never should have moved to the city, it's not good for them. Their health has always been poor, but living in all that smog and smoke with their lung condition is simply idiotic."

I smile at her choice of words. She's right. My husbands are idiots for not living in the countryside where they can be outside without dying from coughing fits. Here, the only thing they have to be careful with is the smoke of the fireplace, but as long as the wood is nice and dry, it doesn't affect them.

"Now, let's wrap those presents," Aunt Laura says and points at the chest again. I smile, now a lot more enthusiastic about the upcoming celebration.

* * *

THE SERVANTS HAVE BEEN SENT home, each of them with a box of goodies to open the day after Christmas. The new cook doesn't start until after the holidays, so our Christmas meal is simple, but still more opulent than what we would have had back home.

A large plate of roast beef is surrounded by bowls of vegetables and a basket with thick slices of bread. I pour yet another helping of the most delicious gravy over my food.

"Are you trying to teach your meat to swim?" Andrew asks with a laugh.

I grin and wave my spoon at him. "It's not my fault the gravy is so good. It would be a waste not to eat it all."

"Eat as much as you want, dear," Aunt Laura says, smiling widely. "There's more gravy in the kitchen."

I raise an eyebrow at Andrew and continue eating my gravy-drenched vegetables.

AFTER LUNCH, we retire to the sitting room and sit around the fireplace. Dan pours the men some whisky and a gin for both Aunt Laura and myself. I can't drink much alcohol, it messes with my machine parts for some reason, but a little gin won't hurt, I'm sure.

Before he sits down, Luke takes something from the mantlepiece and hands it to me. It's a small bronze box, simple and unremarkable. I look up before opening it. All three man are staring at me expectantly.

"Open it before they combust in excitement," Aunt Laura says drily. "I can't stand the tension."

I smile and take the lid off. Inside are four rings, the same colour as the box, but so much more special. Tiny cogs are soldered together to form the rings, then twisted and entwined until it looks like they're grating against each other.

I take the smallest of the rings and hold it up to see it closer. Small traces of silver decorate the cogs, almost imperceptible until light hits the metal and they begin to sparkle.

"It's beautiful," I gasp, slowly putting it on my ring finger.

"Wait until you've seen the best part," Dan says and holds out his hand. "Give us ours."

I hand out the other three rings until we're each wearing one. The men get up and Andrew pulls me to my feet.

"Give me your hand," he whispers and I do as he asks. As soon as our skin touches, the ring begins to quiver, shaking slightly on my finger.

"What's going on?" I ask but Luke interrupts me by wrapping his hand around mine from below, his fingers touching that of his brother. The ring's vibrations increase, making my entire arm tremble. It's a strange feeling, but not uncomfortable.

"And finally, me," Dan says and curls his fingers around my wrist.

Suddenly, the cogs of my ring begin to turn, first slowly, then faster until they reach a steady rhythm. It's not a steady movement, no, it's a pulse, a sound that reminds me of something.

The sound of a beating heart. A human heart.

"We didn't have a ring for you when we got married," Andrew explains. "But that gave us the time to find the perfect one."

Their rings are turning as well, the cogs fitting perfectly together.

Just like us.

"Happy Christmas," they say as one and when I look up into their eyes, I know that I'm the luckiest woman in the world.

THE END

I hope you enjoyed this story! Flip the page to find a list of all my books.
Don't want to miss my upcoming releases? Subscribe to my newsletter:
skyemackinnon.com/newsletter

ABOUT THE AUTHOR

Skye MacKinnon is a USA Today & International Bestselling Author whose books are filled with strong heroines who don't have to choose.

She embraces her Scottishness with fantastical Scottish settings and a dash of mythology, no matter if she's writing about Celtic gods, cat shifters, or the streets of Edinburgh.

When she's not typing away at her favourite cafe, Skye loves dried mango, as much exotic tea as she can squeeze into her cupboards, and being covered in pet hair by her two bunnies, Emma and Darwin.

Support her on Patreon and get exclusive benefits:
patreon.com/skyemackinnon

Subscribe to her newsletter:
skyemackinnon.com/newsletter

- facebook.com/skyemackinnonauthor
- twitter.com/skye_mackinnon
- instagram.com/skyemackinnonauthor
- bookbub.com/authors/skye-mackinnon
- goodreads.com/SkyeMacKinnon
- amazon.com/author/skye_mackinnon

www.ingramcontent.com/pod-product-compliance
Lightning Source LLC
Chambersburg PA
CBHW022255010125
19781CB00007B/238